# Queen Victoria's Knickers

WN

Jackie French &
Bruce Whatley

First published in hardback in Australia by HarperCollins Publishers Pty Ltd in 2010
First published in paperback in Great Britain by HarperCollins Children's Books in 2011

1 3 5 7 9 10 8 6 4 2

ISBN: 978-0-00-741831-2

HarperCollins Children's Books is a division of HarperCollins Publishers Ltd.

Text copyright © Jackie French 2010
Illustrations copyright © Farmhouse Illustration Company Pty Limited 2010

Visit our website at: www.harpercollins.co.uk
Printed and bound in China

To Bruce, Lisa, Jennifer and Natalie, with love and enormous gratitude…
playing with royal underwear has never been so much fun.
JF


For Lisa, who keeps me busy enough to afford clean underwear every day.
BW

M y friend Sam's uncle

used his **secret weapon**

in the fight against Napoleon.

MY friend William's grandpa

helped Captain
Cook find Australia!

MY friend Bridget's father

drove the first steam train in England!

But MY mum made
Queen Victoria's knickers!

Queen Victoria was Empress
of half the world.

She owned palaces and
huge armies. Mighty sultans
gave her precious jewels.

But she didn't have
any knickers.

Most people in those
days didn't wear any
knickers at all.

'The Queen wants my knickers!'

shrieked Mum, when a footman from the palace brought the message.

'Oh, my goodness!' cried Gran.

'Not Mum's knickers, Gran,' I said. 'The ones she makes!'

My mum made the BEST knickers in the world.

Gran sniffed.
'I don't approve of knickers.
If a girl wears proper petticoats
and takes ladylike steps,
she doesn't need knickers.'

'What if the wind blows the Queen's skirt up?'
demanded my brother Bertie.

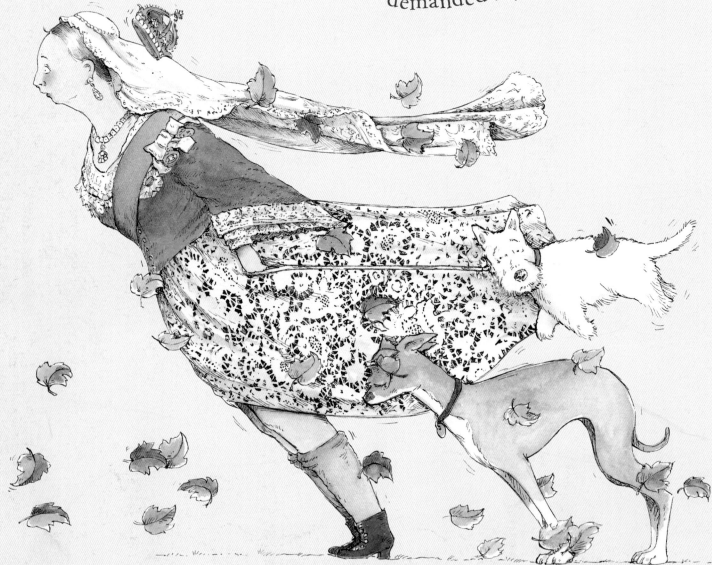

'What if the Queen goes roller-skating?' I asked.

Gran glared at me. 'Her Majesty
NEVER goes roller-skating,' she said.

'Maybe that's because she doesn't have
knickers,' I pointed out.

Mum looked worried.
'What **kind** of knickers
would the Queen like?'

'TARTAN!' cried Bertie.
'The Queen loves tartan – and bagpipes.

They could be bagpipe
knickers. So they play music
when she sits down!'

'They should be **balloon** knickers,' I declared.

'So she can fly across her Empire.'

'Well, they should certainly be well padded and comfortable,' stated Gran, who was starting to become interested.

'It's so difficult!' cried Mum.
'Silk or linen,
lace or frills,
long, short or knee-length?
And what colour?
Who knows what Her Majesty would like!'

'Don't worry, Mum,'
I said. 'We'll all help.'

Dad and Bertie found the finest linen, which came from Ireland.

'Linen is tough, but it's soft, too,' Dad told us.

'We can't give the Queen knickers that could split or make her itch!'

Gran and I visited the lacemakers.

'I need the **best lace** in England,' ordered Gran as the lacemakers twirled their bobbins.

'It's for knickers – for Her Majesty!'

Bertie and I had our own ideas.

'I think the Queen's knickers should
have a secret pocket,' said Bertie,
'to hold cake if she gets hungry,
or to keep bones in for her dogs.'

Mum looked doubtful.

'I'd hate Her Majesty to get
ants in her pants,' she said.

'Well, I think she needs a built-in **warming pan**,' interrupted Gran. 'That palace looks cold and draughty to me.'

'I think her knickers' pockets should have **bows and arrows**,' I said, 'so she can shoot anyone who tries to assassinate her!'

Dad smiled. 'They'd be awfully prickly when she sat down.'

But Mum had already begun
to cut out the knickers.
She cut out one pair,
then another
**and another**
**and another** . . .
until we had fifty-two
pairs of knickers.

We all helped Mum to sew and
then Gran embroidered them
with numbers, so that the Queen
wouldn't get them mixed up.
I embroidered a crown and the
Queen's initials on every pair,
so that no one could ever wear
Her Majesty's knickers
by mistake.

When Queen Victoria was due
to open Parliament that year,
we all had new underwear, too.

Even Gran wore knickers
for the occasion!

But we couldn't help feeling
it was a shame no one would
see any knickers.

'Maybe a **tiger** will escape
from the zoo and tear off the
Queen's skirt!' I cried.

'Or maybe she will fall over,'
suggested Bertie hopefully,
'so everyone will see her
new knickers.'

But then the Queen appeared,
at the front of a long procession.

She wore satin
and diamonds
and rubies
and lace.

She also wore my
mum's knickers –
and a secret smile.

It was the smile of a
woman who knows that
no matter what, no one
will EVER see …

anything they shouldn't . . .

# Author's Note

Very few women wore knickers at the beginning of Queen Victoria's reign in 1837. But the young Queen loved walking, riding, archery and dancing – all the active things that a well-brought-up girl couldn't do for fear of showing something 'rude'. Queen Victoria's championing of knickers helped women achieve a lot more freedom. Just as the Queen made tartans, prams and Christmas trees fashionable, by the time she died in 1901 just about every woman in Britain wore knickers like hers. In one way, Queen Victoria's knickers assisted the birth of women's liberation. Women could even ride the new 'bicycles' and still look perfectly respectable.

Early knickers were also called 'drawers' and then later, 'pantaloons' or 'bloomers' (named after US women's activist, Amelia Bloomer). They were big and bulky and hid the shape of the legs and hips.

The Queen's cypher (monogram) was always included on each item of her underclothing. The cypher consisted of a crown with 'VR' (Victoria Regina) below it and below that a number.

The numbers probably allowed the knickers to be worn in rotation, so that they'd wear out evenly, and so that no one would ever give the Queen a pair of unwashed knickers by accident. We don't know how often the royal washing was done in those days, but the Queen would have needed many pairs of knickers so that she could always have clean ones. Wealthy households had their washing done sometimes only once or twice a year. They looked down on people who were so poor they had to do their washing every week because they didn't have enough fresh clothes. It's possible that many people didn't change their underwear very often!

A pair of Queen Victoria's knickers is on display at the Museum of London, although they are a pair she wore late in life, between 1895 and 1900, when she was much fatter and wore plain clothing instead of the bright colours she loved when her husband was alive. The knickers are made from soft white linen, and are knee-length and buttoned. And despite their age, the fabric hasn't yellowed.